Little Miss Muffet's Big Scare

Crabtree Publishing Company
www.crabtreebooks.com
1-800-387-7650

PMB 59051, 350 Fifth Ave.
59th Floor,
New York, NY 10118

616 Welland Ave.
St. Catharines, ON
L2M 5V6

Published by Crabtree Publishing in 2013

Series editor: Louise John
Editors: Katie Powell, Kathy Middleton
Notes to adults: Reagan Miller
Cover design: Paul Cherrill
Design: D.R.ink
Consultant: Shirley Bickler
Production coordinator and
   Prepress technician: Margaret Amy Salter
Print coordinator: Katherine Berti

Text © Alan Durant 2009
Illustration © Leah-Ellen Heming 2009

First published in
2009 by Wayland
(A division of Hachette
Children's Books)

Printed in Hong Kong/
092012/BK20120629

**Library and Archives Canada
Cataloguing in Publication**

CIP available at Library and Archives Canada

**Library of Congress
Cataloging-in-Publication Data**

CIP available at Library of Congress

Little Miss Muffet's Big Scare

Written by Alan Durant
Illustrated by Leah-Ellen Heming

Crabtree Publishing Company

www.crabtreebooks.com

Little Miss Muffet was a girl with a curl in the middle of her forehead.

When she was bad she was very, very bad, and when she was good...well, she was never good. She was always horrid.

She loved to sit on her tuffet and play nasty tricks on everyone. One day, Doctor Foster came and asked the way to Gloucester.

Little Miss Muffet said, "It's that way," and pointed him toward the biggest, deepest puddle you ever did see.

Poor Doctor Foster stepped into water right up to his middle!

One night, the Man in the Moon tumbled down on his way to shine on Norwich. Little Miss Muffet was sitting on her tuffet, eating from a bowl.

"That looks nice," said the Man in the Moon. "What is it?"
"It's cold pease porridge," said Little Miss Muffet.

8

"Oooh!" exclaimed the Man in the Moon.
"That's my favorite!"
"Try some," said Little Miss Muffet
smiling, and she handed him the bowl.

But the pease porridge wasn't cold. It was
so hot it burned the Man in the Moon's
mouth. "Ow!" he yelled.

When Jack moaned that he had fallen down a hill and cut his head, Little Miss Muffet told him to pour vinegar on it, and wrap it in brown paper.

Well, of course, all that did was make
the cut sting even more and make Jack
look very silly. Little Miss Muffet laughed
and laughed.

The worst trick that Little Miss Muffet played was on Mrs. Ladybug. She told her that her house was on fire and her children were alone.

Poor Mrs. Ladybug nearly had a heart attack—and, of course, it wasn't true.

What a wicked, wicked girl Little Miss Muffet was.

Finally, everyone had had enough.
"It's time we taught that wicked girl
a lesson," they said.

The first to try was Georgie Porgie.
"I'll kiss her," he said. "That'll make
her cry. Girls always cry when I
kiss them."

But Little Miss Muffet didn't cry. She laughed and stuck out her tongue at Georgie Porgie, which made HIM cry.

She hissed and snarled at Little Miss Muffet, but the bad little girl just laughed.

Then she roared at Pussy Cat and chased HER away.

"I know what to do with bad children," said the old woman who lived in a shoe. "I've got lots of them."

But Little Miss Muffet was too quick for the old woman. She grabbed the old woman's stick and chased her with it. Then she broke it in two.

There was only one thing left to do. It was time to call for the scariest person of all— the man who gave everybody the shivers– Doctor Fell! Surely HE could scare Little Miss Muffet.

Doctor Fell went to see Little Miss Muffet.
He stared at her with his beady eyes.
He smiled his scary crooked grin.
He opened his bag of nightmares
and took out a black bottle.

"Try some of my lovely medicine,"
he croaked.
"Thanks," chirped Little Miss Muffet.

She took a big swig, then spit
it out all over Doctor Fell!
"I'm not scared of you," she laughed.

Little Miss Muffet sat on her tuffet, eating her favorite dish of curds and whey—and feeling very pleased with herself.

26

"I'm not scared of anything," she said.
But she was wrong.

Suddenly, an itsy bitsy spider appeared out of a waterspout next to her tuffet.

It crept over to Little Miss Muffet and sat down beside her.

Little Miss Muffet turned and...
"Arghhh! A spider!" she shrieked.

She jumped up and threw her bowl
in the air.

Then she ran away as fast as she could, screaming her head off.

And, from that day on, she has never been seen again!

Notes for adults

Tadpoles: Nursery Crimes are structured for transitional and early fluent readers. The books may also be used for read-alouds or shared reading with younger children.

Tadpoles: Nursery Crimes are intended for children who are familiar with nursery rhyme characters and themes, but can also be enjoyed by anyone. Each story can be compared with the traditional rhyme, or appreciated for its own unique twist.

IF YOU ARE READING THIS BOOK WITH A CHILD, HERE ARE A FEW SUGGESTIONS:

1. Make reading fun! Choose a time to read when you and the child are relaxed and have time to share the story.

2. Before reading, invite the child to preview the book. The child can read the title, look at the illustrations, skim through the text, and make predictions as to what will happen in the story. This activity stimulates curiosity and promotes critical thinking skills.

3. During reading, encourage the child to monitor his or her understanding by asking questions to draw conclusions, making connections, and using context clues to understand unfamiliar words.

4. After reading, ask the child to review his or her predictions. Were they correct? Discuss different parts of the story, including main characters, setting, main events, the problem and solution. Challenge the child to retell the story in his or her own words to enhance comprehension.

5. Give praise! Children learn best in a positive environment.

VISIT THE LIBRARY AND CHECK OUT THESE RELATED NURSERY RHYMES AND CHILDREN'S SONGS:

Little Miss Muffet
There Was a Little Girl
Doctor Foster

Pease Pudding Hot
Jack and Jill
Ladybug Ladybug

Georgie Porgie
There Was an Old Woman Who Lived in a Shoe

IF YOU ENJOYED THIS BOOK, WHY NOT TRY ANOTHER TADPOLES: NURSERY CRIMES STORY?

Humpty Dumpty's Great Fall   *978-0-7787-8028-1 RLB*   *978-0-7787-8039-7 PB*
Little Bo Peep's Missing Sheep   *978-0-7787-8029-8 RLB*   *978-0-7787-8040-3 PB*
Old Mother Hubbard's Stolen Bone   *978-0-7787-8031-1 RLB*   *978-0-7787-8042-7 PB*

VISIT WWW.CRABTREEBOOKS.COM FOR OTHER CRABTREE BOOKS.